To Jane
A dear friend and
an excellent supervisor
Barbara Leiter
1989

THE ANGEL OF MUDDY RIVER

THE ANGEL OF MUDDY RIVER

by

Barbara Reiter

A Geneva Book

Carlton Press, Inc. New York, N.Y.

Manufactured in the United States of America
ISBN 0-8062-2995-0

THE ANGEL OF MUDDY RIVER

Some of the little rodents "barked" their displeasure as the small grullo carefully picked his way through the prairie dog town.

The tiny gray horse and his master were coated with trail dust. They had traveled several days in this arid land, with little grass and less water. It has been a long hard journey to reach this remote area.

The horse's master dozed in the saddle. He left the task of getting through this prairie dog town to the nimble-footed mustang.

A scent of fresh water from the distant river caught the horse's nostrils. The thought of good grass and fresh water hurried the tough little range horse along. His gait changed from a slow cautious walk to a spirited lope. As the mustang literally flew through the buffalo grass the change of gait rudely awakened his rider.

The long-strided lope of the mustang cut the distance to the river. Reaching the river both horse and rider enjoyed a long cool drink. Afterwards, the horse's master made camp, and enjoyed his first good night's sleep in more than a week.

Morning found the grullo fiesty and full of himself. It took strong hands to guide the young bronc across the fast rolling river. Having reached the far shore, the mustang stopped and shook the water from his hide.

His master dismounted, pulled off the saddle and blanket to let them dry before going on. Reaching down to grab the saddle and blanket, he noticed wagon tracks. It was odd that a wagon train would come this way. The mountains in the distance were sheer and jagged. No wagon could cross them. It was almost impossible to get a horse and rider across them. Most of the wagon trails ran far to the north. Yet, it was the horseman's good fortune that a train had came this way.

He was a gunman by profession. His last job was interrupted when the calvary was called in. The rancher that had hired him paid him in full, but he had dared not stop for supplies. Quickly, he resaddled the mustang, and followed the wagon tracks as they traveled further into the shadows of the mountains. The tracks were about a day old, he guessed. He never had been able to figure out the age of tracks. He followed the tracks until dark. Making a fire in one of the pits made by members of the wagon train, he sat down and enjoyed a smoke.

For the second night in a row he enjoyed another night's rest. The thought of having a good meal tomorrow made his sleep more restful.

Dawn found him back on the trail. He'd made himself a promise that morning, as he cinched his belt up another notch, he'd catch up with that train today no matter how fast they traveled. He traveled several hours, then suddenly the mustang snorted. At first, he thought the animal had gotten dust in his nose. The little grullo was always rank, but now he was almost more than the gunman could handle. Fighting to take the bit in his teeth, the grullo reared and tossed his head violently. His master snapped up the reins, jerking the steed's head sharply. Then the rider raked him roughly with the rowel spurs. Once again the animal calmed, but was sidestepping and snorting.

The sun was blindingly bright, and squinting the gunman missed the object on the ground. His mount didn't. The little horse squealed with fright, and not even the strong hands of the rider could not hold him. It did not take long for the gunman to check the bolting horse. The tough little animal was trembling with fright. Turning the horse toward the object on the ground proved nearly an impossible task.

Finally, he dismounted and walked toward the object, leading the reluctant mustang with him. As the horse snorted and blowed behind him, he realized that what had spooked the horse, had been human at one time. The gunman had seen a lot of grim and grotesque sights, but nothing like this.

This poor soul had made somebody crazy, for only the insane would do something like this. He backed away from the man, and felt sick and weak. When the horse realized they were leaving, he moved quickly away from there.

They traveled only a short distance, when the tops of the

wagons came into view. He heard a whinny from one of their horses first. As he cleared the brush he saw the camp, or what was left of it.

Again the little mustang jumped with fright, and each forward step was a battle. Men, women and children lay dead throughout the camp. Some of the women still held their babies in death as they had in life. Several of the wagons had been overturned. Most of the animals had been ran off. Leaving behind only the dead and injuried.

He had not heard any gunshots, but now he knew why. There were only a couple of muzzle loaders in camp, and the travelers had been killed by knife or sword. These people, though dead, were lucky. None had suffered the same torture as the man he'd found earlier. Mercifully, he shot several of the horses that had suffered broken legs in the attack.

There were too many people to bury, but he could not leave the children for the buzzards. He began placing the children in one of the wagons. There was enough fuel oil in their supplies to soak one of the wagons and burn it. This was perhaps the most unpleasant task he'd ever undertaken. Whoever was responsible would pay for this.

Slowly, almost cautiously he moved the children's cold, stiff lifeless bodies to the wagon. A wagon had overturned on one girl, pinning half her body under it. He was going to leave her, but decided not to. Taking his lasso from the saddle, he slipped it on the wagon's brake handle and righted the wagon.

Ground-tying the little grullo, he picked up the girl's body. The girl's body was limp. Suddenly, he realized her body was afire with fever. The girl was alive. That huge wagon should have crushed her, yet it didn't. He noticed an ugly stab wound under her rib cage.

Carefully, he placed her on the ground. Kneeling, he removed her bonnet and felt her forehead. It was hot, like the coals in a dying fire. Ripping the canvas from one of the wagons, and placing it on planks torn from the side of a wagon, he quickly made a travois.

He snatched up the reins of a black Percheron, that had been cut in the raid. The huge draft horse had a deep slash across its chest. He hitched the Percheron to the travois. Gently, he picked the girl up and placed her on the travois. He covered her with a blanket, and packed extra supplies that he had salvaged on the horse drawn stretcher with the girl.

Before leaving he set fire to the wagon with the children bodies in it. The last thing he needed was a kid slowing him down, yet at no time did he consider leaving her.

They traveled very slowly back to the river. He found shelter there under an overhanging rock. Reaching the shelter, he left the horses and the injured girl long enough to cut some evergreen boughs to make their beds. After carrying the branches back to the campsite, he found plenty of dry wood for a camp fire. He put the evergreen limbs in two stacks and covered them with blankets.

He felt the young girl's face. She was burning up with fever. She was deathly hot. He lifted her from the travois and onto the bed of limbs. Pulling his hunting knife from it's sheath on his thigh, he cut away her dress, by the stab wound. He found an ugly festering sore.

Getting a pan from his saddlebags, he filled it with water from his canteen, and placed it on the fire. The girl began to shake as he waited for the water to heat.

During the War of the Rebellion, he had watched both of his younger brothers do the same thing before they died. Almost in a panic, he snatched up the girl's body and ran for the river. He ran into the river still carrying her. The water was swift and ice cold, yet he waded in waist deep.

Holding her with one hand he ripped the dress loose first from one shoulder, and then from the other. He gripped both of her shoulders firmly, to avoid her head being swept under in the swift current. Disregarding the ice cold water, he stood there and held her burning body under for a long time.

Finally, he scooped up the girl in his arms and carried her out of the river. Getting to shore, he wrapped her bare body in a blanket. He got back in his pack, and pulled out his spare shirt. After drying her body with the blanket, he put his shirt on her. It fit her almost like a dress.

Turning, he placed his hunting knife's blade into the fire. Soon the blade was hot, and with deft, quick hands he opened the injured place on her side. It did not take long to bandage the wound after it had been opened and cleaned. Finishing his task, he sat back and rolled himself a smoke, and wished for a drink. He needed it.

Shortly, he reached over and felt her forehead. It was warm, but not deathly hot.

Leaning back against the rocks of the overhang, he tossed some more wood onto the fire. The fire flamed up as the new wood was added. This sudden burst of sparks, spooked the little mustang. Christian got up and walked to the horses. He unsaddled the grullo, and removed the travois from the Percheron. With dried grass he rubbed down both animals. Staking the mustang out to graze for the evening finished his task. The Percheron wouldn't wander far.

He ate some jerky he'd found at the wagon train's camp. Several times, while he was eating, he glanced over and looked at the wounded girl. She was struggling to survive.

If the kid lived, she'd need food. He'd hunt in the morning, and if that failed he'd go fishing. He leaned back and rolled himself a smoke.

The rest of the night he sat there and watched the injured girl. There were several times that he thought she had died, but then he'd notice the blanket move as she breathed. By dawn her fever had broke, but she was very weak.

He went hunting and within a short time he'd killed two prairie chickens. As he returned to their camp, he noticed the girl was moving some. It was only a few minutes later that she opened her eyes for the first time since he'd found her. Pain caused her to grit her teeth, and grab her side.

Quickly and with an uncommon gentleness, he grasped her hands in one of his. Kneeling beside her he stroked her head with the other hand. In a soft, reassuring tone he told her that she was safe. Her eyes closed and she slept again. Late in the afternoon, she opened her eyes again. He had boiled the game birds and fed her the broth. She ate only a couple of sips, but he was pleased. It was a beginning.

The next several days she spent asleep most of the time. At no time did she speak. Several times she would begin to toss while sleeping as the nightmare she survived returned.

Nearly a week past before she regained any strength. "Good morning," he greeted as she awoke.

Her color was returning, and this morning for the first time she smiled at his greeting. The smile quickly faded as the pain returned. This did not upset the gunman. He was delighted that she smiled.

Once again he kneeled beside her. Again he spoke with an unusual gentleness. "Angel," he began, "my name's Christian Daniels. My friends call me Chris, and you are safe here." She looked at him with her big blue eyes as though not certain of him. There was an uneasy frighten look in her eyes. "Angel," he continued, "you want to tell me what happened?"

Slowly the sad and horrifying story began to unfold. "I was traveling to King's Fork with other members of the followers." She began. "I was to be..."here she hesitated.

"To be what?" asked the gunman.

Blushing, it was the first time he'd seen real color in her face, she answered, "....Mar—ried."

"Married?" he questioned in almost a harsh tone. "To who?"

"Brother Zebadiah agreed to marry me," she said weakly.

"Agreed?!" asked the gunman rudely. "How old are you, girl?"

"I'm fourteen." She answered. It was the man that gritted his teeth this time, but held his tongue. "Brother Isaac formed a group of our neighbors to travel to King's Fork. That's where the settlement of followers is located. Brother Zebadiah built the settlement there about ten years ago.

"Angel, how old is this Brother Zebadiah?" asked the man beside her.

"I...I...I don't know," she said, "but, he's a DEACON!"

Unimpressed the gunman said, "Go on."

"All the followers sold their farms, and gave the money to Brother Isaac. It was Brother Isaac that made the arrangement for me to marry Brother Zebadiah. Brother Zebadiah's wife died while Brother Isaac was at King's Fork to make the arrangements for the followers to arrive. He knew my Grandpap was my only kin and that he wanted to return to the old country. So when he came back from King's Fork he gave Grandpap enough money to make the trip, and I was to marry Brother Zebadiah."

Daniels sat there silently. He did not like what he was hearing. These so-called holy men apparently bought this young girl. That did not sit right with him. Daniels frowned as the girl continued her story.

"We got to St. Joe in just a couple of weeks. We were to join a big train that was forming there, and travel with them till we reached the King's Fork's turn off. It was in St. Joe where Brother Isaac's met Brother William. Brother William told us that we could reach King's Fork in half the time if we didn't follow the main trail."

"And your Brother Isaac believed him?" questioned Daniels.

"Yes," she answered innocently. "Brother William offered to show us the way. He said that he was headed in that general direction, and would help us."

"Did your Brother William have a last name?" asked the gunman.

"I..I don't remember....yes, it was Coulter." she said

"WILLIE COULTER!!!" shouted Daniels. "I shoulda known," continued the gunman in a rage. "I should of killed that son of a bitch two years ago," he growled.

"But, Brother William tried to help," defended the girl. "Even after the raid began he tried to help, him and Brother Isaac took the money box to hide it."

Then it was Brother Isaac that had spooked the grullo when he first arrived at the wagon train. Everything made sense now. That was Willie Coulter's style, and he should of known it when he found the body.

"I...I...I don't remember no more...except..some screaming in the distance, but it was real far way," she said as tears filled her eyes.

He pulled her toward him, and held the girl in his arms, comforting her. The weary girl closed her eyes and was asleep as he tucked her in. He watched her sleep, she wasn't more than a child. Some old man paying for her, thought the gunman. He'd pay hell before he got this one.

Later, she awoke and ate some rabbit that he'd cooked. "This Brother Zebadiah, he gonna be looking for ya?" asked Daniels.

"No, I don't think so," she answered.

"Are you in love with him?" questioned the gunman.

Blushing a dark reddish-purple, she shook her head. "No." Then looking down as though ashamed she said, "I've never met him." Then with total innocence that shook the gunman's very marrow she said, "I hope he like's me."

"King's Fork's out of my way," angrily snapped Daniels. "What am I gonna do with you?"

The little blonde haired girl sat there silently and listened to his angry words. When he finished she looked at him and spoke. "I'm sorry! I know I'm a burden to you!" Then she started to get to her feet. But stopped as the burning rage in her side became unbearable. The color left her face as her face twisted with pain and suddenly King's Fork was no longer out of Daniels way.

"Hey! Sit down!" ordered Daniels. "You wanta rip that side open?" he asked. She shook her head no as she obeyed.

The next couple of days found her much stronger, and she spent more time sitting up.

"Do you think you'll be able to travel?" he asked.

"Yes,", she answered without hesitation.

"Girl, you best wear these for traveling," he said as he tossed her trousers and a shirt.

"I can't..." she blushed. "They're boys' clothes."

"You can and YOU WILL!" snapped Daniels. "If'n you don't put them on, so help me, I'll put 'em on you myself!"

His order cleared the color from her face. Stark fear replaced embarrassment. "Yes, sir." She answered meekly as she obeyed.

He took the two horses and walked to the river to let them drink. When he returned, she was dressed and ready to go. He gave her a leg up on the draft horse. She rode with only a blanket to protect the horse's back.

The grullo, with his long rest and good feed, was full of himself. The little grullo bucked, twisted, sunfished and jumped. As the girl watched, Daniels met each move with the skill of a master. Finally the rank mustang had had enough and settled down.

As ornery as the little beast was, Christian Daniels would never part with him. The mustang was dependable, in a land of undependable factors. It had been this little horse that had stayed with him when he'd been ambushed by Apaches. It was this same little horse that had killed a rattlesnake not more than a few inches from striking his hand as he slept. And it was the same little horse that had made such a ruckus; when horse thieves tried to run off his friend, Jake Karcher's horses, that had awaken the bunk house and the ranch house crew. Daniels would never admit it, but he depended on the little mustang.

With the grullo behaving himself now, the gunman reached over and grabbed the draft horse's reins. They traveled less than half a day before the girl began to lean on the draft horse's neck.

Almost too late, he realized she was weaker than he had suspected.

Pulling the mustang up short, he swung out of the saddle and walked to the draft horse. He reached up and with a gentle tug, pulled her over and as she slid off the horse's back she went into his arms. Leaning her against a tree stump he let her rest. It was dawn before they headed on again. This time he placed her in the little range horse's saddle and he rode on the bedroll behind the saddle.

Daniels knew there was a good chance the little mustang might throw one of his bucking fits. However, to his surprise, the grullo seemed to realize the need for gentleness. He showed manners totally alien to his normal behavior.

Again they traveled very slowly, as the girl remained weak, yet she did not complain.

Christian Daniels had not realized her wound had opened, until he noticed her hands gripping the saddlehorn. Her knuckles were white. Immediately he pulled up the grullo. Again, he helped her off the horse and let her rest. He rebandaged the wound.

Finally he built a fire and made some coffee.

She slept for several hours and when she awoke, she wanted to travel again.

"You got people back east?" he asked.

"No. Not anymore," she answered. "My grandpap was all I had an he was going back to the old country," said the girl.

"Look," he began hesitantly. "Listen!" he continued. "If I get you your fare home, would you go?"

"Home?" she questioned.

"Look, that Zebadiah you're to hitch to, well...maybe...maybe he ain't gonna wantta marry ya. Why he'll be wantin' you to be having babies, and you won't have the strength for that for sometime."

There it was out, and he'd got it said. It was harder for him to say that to the girl, than it would have been for him to take twenty lashes with a blacksnake whip.

This was the longest speech and most personal talk he'd ever had with a woman. He'd been upstairs with saloon girls and he'd slept with a rancher's daughter a time or two or more, but he'd never talked personal to them. He'd just told them he loved them, and stuff they wanted to hear. This was different. He was talking to his "Angel" and she was different.

He found himself feeling responsible for her. He'd not been responsible for anything or anyone, but himself for a long time. This new responsibility made him uncomfortable.

The girl was quiet for a long time and then she said, "I...I have to marry...marry him, it's been arranged." This infuriated the gunman, but he said nothing for fear of frightening the girl even more

The sun was setting when they stopped for the evening. He built the fire, but for the first time since he'd found her, she cooked their supper. It was a good meal and filling.

He changed the bandage on her wound and finally it appeared to be healing. It was only a short time later till she was asleep by the fire.

He rolled himself a smoke, but never lit it. The events of the past several weeks had left him drained. It was nice to turn in early too.

* * *

The flames in the fire had all but faded when her screams awakened him, and frightened the horses. He grabbed her and shook her awake. She trembled in his arm as the nightmare faded. He pulled her to him and held her as her body trembled.

"Sh..hu..hu," he said gently.

But this did not stop her from saying, "They're all dead! Sally...Beth Ann...Bertha...Homer...Karl" she pushed away from Daniels and looked at him with eyes that could have melted a colder heart, than his. "They're all dead!"

Slowly he nodded, confirming their fate. She continued to look at him for a minute and then as her eyes welled with tears, her voice broke as she asked, "Why did they all have to die?"

Then she cried. He had never felt so helpless before in his life. He just grabbed her again, and locked her young body in his arms and let her cry it out.

Tears welled in his eyes as he held her, for the first time since he'd buried his brothers during the war. It was almost dawn before she finally dozed off into a troubled sleep. He didn't feel like sleeping, he should've killed that bastard Coulter two years ago when he had the chance.

The girl slept late, but the morning brought a bright sun and a better mood for her. They headed out without breakfast, and the girl seemed much better today. Yet, Daniels would not risk her injury and stopped frequently to let her rest.

"Do you know anyone at all at King's Fork?" asked Christian Daniels.

"No, Mr. Daniels," she answered meekly.

"You call me Chris, okay?" he said. She said nothing, but her smile needed no words.

"What is your name?" he asked.

"My name's Libby Ward," said the girl in response to his question.

"Miss Libby, you don't have to marry nobody that you don't want," said the gunman. The idea of her being bought for marriage still was an open sore and the thought of it only rubbed salt in the wound.

"...but, I'm obligated," she said. "My Grandpap said I gotta."

This riled Daniels, "HELL! Let your 'Grandpap' marry the old fool!" She giggled at the thought.

It was the first time he'd heard her laugh and he liked the sound of it.

"I'll send you back east," stated Daniels.

The girl was quiet for a long time and then said, "I ain't got nothin' to go back for." Then seeming to accept her fate she said, "It might'n be so bad."

This angered her rescuer. Yet, it was useless to try and talk her out of it. He got even madder at himself for getting involved.

They reached the top of a rise and saw a trading post ahead.

It took only a short time to reach the frontier outpost. They stopped at the hitch rail. She was just stepping to the ground when two grizzled men came out of the trading post.

Chritian Daniels had given her a hand down. Now as she saw the strangers, her grip on his arm suddenly tightened. He felt her whole body quiver. He slid the leather loop from the hammer of his gun, as he whispered to her. "I won't let them hurt you." "Libby, do you reckonize them?" he asked.

Shaking her head, she answered, "They all looked the same."

"Well com'on," he urged, "we'll go inside." She hesitated, but he gently coaxed her in. Again he showed a gentleness most unusual in his nature.

She had never seen such a place. Everything was stacked up. There were harnesses, wagon parts, and Indian items. She looked at the arrows of the different tribes, blankets and war bonnets.

The trader was a man called Benny Warclaw. He was a short, fat man whose head was totally bald and scarred from when he was scalped. Libby stood there and compared the two men. Chris was just the opposite. Daniels was at least six foot, he was lean and leatherly, he had thick almost shoulder-length black hair and cold dark brown eyes. His shoulder were broad, and he walked without fear.

Her thoughts were interrupted by the trader.

"You seen any wagon train tracks, or any sign of some wagons?" asked the man called Benny Warclaw.

"Train in this part of the country?" asked the gunman. "Naw, I ain't seen none, and don't expect to either."

"Heard one was coming," said the trader. "Ain't seen it, and it ain't never got here."

"Well I ain't seen no wagons moving," said the gunman.

The girl still dressed in 'boy's clothes' stood by the door and waited for Daniels. It was as she stood there that she saw a spinning wheel that Mrs. Packer was taking with her to their new home at King's Fork.

As Daniels prepared to leave, he asked Libby if she needed anything. It was then that she whispered to him about the spinning wheel.

"Sh..h..h," said the gunman shaking his head no.

"BOY WANT SOMPTHING!?!" shouted the trader in broken English.

"No," said Daniels in response, as he kept between the trader and the girl. Gently he pushed her toward the door.

Suddenly she stopped. Reaching into a stack of blankets and quilts, she pulled one out. "This is mine!" she announced.

To Daniels dismay, she turned and confronted the trader. "This is mine!" she stated again.

The trader was shocked by the tall man's companion's sex. Five dollars and it's yours," said the trader rudely.

"It ain't got no money," said the girl honestly.

Then YOU got no blanket!" answered the trader snatching the quilt from her hands.

As the trader succeeded in retreiving his merchandise, the girl turned on her heel and looked to the man she was with. "It's mine!" she pleaded. It was not her words, but the look in her blue eyes that caused the gunman to slip the leather loop from the gun's hammer again. He wore a single holster slung low on his hip, and the walnut handled colt had seen much use.

The trader realized his peril. It was one thing to snatch a quilt from a girl. It was quite different when the steel-eyed gunman dealt in.

"I'll be taking that with me," stated the gunman.

"Yeah, YOU take it!" agreed Benny Warclaw hastily, as he handed the quilt to the man. Daniels handed the quilt to the girl. Then without moving he urged her out the door. Keeping an eye on the trader, Daniels backed out of the trading post.

Several minutes later, as the trading post seemed only a dot on the plains, the girl spoke. "Thank you," she said.

Daniels smiled. The girl did not see him, as he still had her sit in his saddle as he rode on the bedroll behind her.

She was feeling much better." "Is it far to King's Fork now?" asked Libby.

"In a hurry to get there?" he asked with a rather rude tone.

"No," she answered truthfully, shaking her blonde hair. "I'm...I'm just a little scared." She said truthfully. Without comment, Daniels tightened his grip on the reins, and in so doing tightened his grip on her.

That evening as they stopped for the night, Libby was more talkative than ever before. "I didn't aim to cause you no trouble back there," she said.

"You didn't," Daniels answered.

Later that evening, in the dim light of the campfire, the gunman fixed his pack of supplies so they could be tied onto the draft horse in the morning. He glanced at the girl, who was sleeping soundly and peacefully on the ground, across from the campfire. She was using the quilt for a pillow.

The crow-feet wrinkles by his eyes moved as his eyes softened and a shadow of a smile crossed his lips at the sight of her.

As the campfire died down, Daniels walked around the outside of the camp to check their safety. When he was certain that all was secure, he returned to camp. Before turning in, he checked on Libby. Gently he pulled her blanket up around her shoulders and tucked it in. There was a bite in the air, and he didn't want her to catch her death.

Morning came early. Christian awoke to the aroma of brewed coffee, fried sow-belly and eggs. "Girl, you start feeding me like this, and I'll be spoiled in no time." He stated.

"I hope you like it, Chris," she said with a little color coming to her face.

Seeing six eggs heaped on his plate he asked, "Did you eat?"

"I ain't hungry," she answered.

"You feeling poorly?" he asked.

No she answered by shaking her head.

"You don't eat enough to keep a bird alive!" growled the gunman. "How in the hell you gonna git your strength back?" he asked.

"I...I...I don't know, "humbly answerd the girl.

"Well, you look too pale to me," stated Daniels. "You need fresh meat."

"I...I don't wantta be no burden," said the girl.

Angrily Chris looked up from his meal. "You keep talking like that, and I'm gonna leave you right here."

"I'm sorry," she apologized.

This only made him more angry with her.

"Young lady," he began in a restrained voice, "NEVER, do you apologize to me. If you got something to say, you say it!"

"Don't you *ever* be afraid to speak up!"

"Angel, you know you don't have to be scared of me, don't you?"

Slowly she raised her head. She looked at Chris. His eyes felt like they could pierce through her soul. His growl sent cold chills down her back, yet deep down she knew she was safer with him than anyone.

Growing impatient, he demanded, "WELL!?!"

A faint smile crossed her lips. "I...I don't know," she answered bashfully.

"Damn girl!" He roared. "I mean you no harm!" Disgustedly he turned and started to walk away. He stopped, turned around, and confronted her. "What is it?" He asked. "You think I'm like those that raided the wagons? Or maybe you think I am one of the raiders!" He accused.

Shaking her head no, she spoke without looking up. "Speak up!" he demanded. "You owe me that much!"

Finally she looked up at him. That frightened doe look was in her eyes. As her voice broke she said, "I...I..I like you." Then finding her courage she continued, "I know you aren't like those others. But..." she paused.

"But what??" he demanded.

"I'm scared," she confessed shamefully.

"Of me!?" he asked.

He watched her intently, and as her lips quivered she began, "Everything's so different. When my Grandpap took that money....I didn't know it was gonna be like this," she explained, lowering her head as though ashamed.

Chris Daniels reached under her chin, and lifted her head with his hand till she was looking at him. "Meal time comes around, we both eat. Okay?" he asked.

She smiled and nodded yes, and he grinned that all was well with them. "Come on, we best be getting along," he said.

"I can take the big horse," she said. "I won't slow you down now."

"No," he said. "You ride behind me on my mustang. He can carry the two of us. "Sides I'll use the other horse to pack."

Sitting atop the bedroll behind the saddle wasn't uncomfortable, and she felt safe with her rescuer.

He still stopped rather frequently for her to rest. She had vastly improved in spirit, and was slowly improving in strength.

Three days they traveled without seeing anyone. On the fourth day they saw an Indian raiding party.

"We best hold up till they clear out," warned Daniels as he slid off the mustang. Quickly he found cover for the horses, the girl and himself.

The girl was terrified, yet she did not complain. She sat there beside him with her head resting on her bent knees and her arms wrapping around her knees. With his rifle in hand, Daniels watched the Indians as they rode across the plains and disappeared over a distant rise.

Silently she had a way of touching his heart as no one had ever done before. As she sat there trembling and fighting back tears, he watched as there was nothing more he could do. Even the tough little mustang walked over by her and lowered his head, as though trying to reassure her that she wasn't alone.

The next day they travelled cautiously. A little after noon they came upon the smoldering remains of a cabin.

"You wait here," he said stopping the grullo a good distance from the cabin. He handed her the lead rope of the draft horse as he dismounted.

"No," she said. "I'd rather stay with you."

"There are probably dead people up there," he warned.

The pale girl spoke, "I figured that." Then with eyes he could not deny, she pleaded. "Please don't leave me here alone."

He reached over and took hold of the grullo's bridle and led the skiddish animal forward. When they reached the cabin's remains, his worst fears were confirmed. There had been several adults and a couple of children. The raiding party had left no survivors.

Libby sat gripping the cantle with both hands, as she tried not to look at the victims. From time to time the gunman would reach up and touch her hands in a supportive way. "We can't do nothing here," said Daniels as he stepped into the saddle.

"You okay?" He asked with concern for the girl. She nodded her head slowly.

* * * * *

They traveled, until darkness made traveling dangerous. He stepped down and reaching his hands up, and grabbing her waist, he lifted her down from the saddle. Gently he sat her down on her feet. He had been careful not to injure the healing wound.

This evening he built the campfire and cooked their supper.

He was worried about the girl, since finding the cabin massacre she had hardly spoken. The color was gone from her face, and her hands were cold. That evening she ate very little, but when she finished she did clean their plates and closed the packs.

As he leaned back against a huge rock, he reached a hand up toward her. "Come here," he said. She sat down next to him. "You look tired," he said.

"I'm okay," she answered, then yawned.

The wind had changed and there was a bite in the wind. "You cold?" he asked.

"Just a little chilly," she answered as she leaned her head

against his arm.

With one arm around her, he reached over with his free hand and grabbed her quilt. Pulling it to them, he gently wrapped it around the girl. She was asleep in moments.

The girl slept soundly. He pulled the makings for a smoke from his pocket. Daniels changed his mind before rolling his smoke. Easily he moved, and shifted her head from his arm to his chest. As she continued to sleep, he leaned over and kissed her hair on the top of her head.

He began to doze off to sleep. Suddenly, he was wide awake. In two days they'd be in King's Fork. Three days from now she'd be gone! He'd never see her again! It was with that thought on his mind that he eventually fell off to sleep.

He had been asleep only a short time when the sound of a twig snapping awoke him. The big draft horse had just stepped on a fallen dried branch. Sleepily, the girl rubbed her eyes and asked what was happening.

"Sh" he whispered as he eased her back against him. It wasn't long until the girl was sound asleep again.

As he carefully moved strands of hair from her face. He thought out loud, "What am I gonna do with you, little one."

Then silently, he thought of the man awaiting his 'bride'...

It was well before daylight when the girl awoke. Daniels had made a fire, while Libby prepared their breakfast.

The two travelers got an early start. They traveled without stopping through out the morning. A butterfly flew in front of the draft horse and it frightened it so bad it squealed. Seeing the whole episode, the girl laughed, even Daniels, who seldom laughed, had a good laugh at the draft horse's plight.

"Oh..h.." said the girl still laughing as she clutched her side. "My side hurts when I laugh."

They stopped shortly to water the horses. "We'll be in King's Fork shortly," announced Daniels.

"I guess you'll be glad when we get there," said the girl.

"Yeah," lied the gunman.

"Will you stay a spell?" she asked.

The gunman shook his head no. Then said, "No...I gotta job waiting for me." She accepted his answer without comment.

They made camp early that night. Libby walked down by the stream, there she bathed and washed her hair. The water was cool, clear and clean. Returning to camp, Daniels asked her if she needed a new bandage on her wound.

"No," she answered. "It's healing nicely. I don't believe it'll need to be bandaged anymore."

"Pain almost gone?" he inquired.

"Yes," she responded. "It only hurts when I laugh."

That night he couldn't get to sleep. He prowled around the camp like a restless cougar. He had a lot on his mind, and he sought answers that did not come easy. Finally, he grabbed his rifle and stood guard over the camp. When he looked at the small sleeping figure, there by the campfire, his eyes softened.

"How long had she been with him, now?" he thought to himself. After a few moments, he shook his head as though it would take the thoughts of her future away.

It was mid-morning when they reached the edge of King's Fork. Daniels pulled the little mustang up. The man and girl both dismounted and walked leading the horses. "Angel," began her rescuer, "if you ever need me, I'll be there." He said with feeling.

She looked at him with a disbelieving look in her eyes. "I wouldn't even know how to get in touch with you," she stated truthfully.

He had hoped King's Fork would be a dirty little settlement, like those that sprang up all over the west. They usually contained a saloon, a cat house, a general store and a few log cabins. If King's Fork was like that, he might be able to convince her to go back east.

To his dismay, the village was just the opposite. The town was a neat little community, with whitewashed board houses, fenced yards and hitching posts instead of rails, there was a church with a steeple, a one-room school house and a well stocked general store. This settlement also contained a blacksmith's shop, and a small inn for travelers. Each of the yards contained beds of flowers, while the backyards each had a huge garden plot.

Children of all ages were everywhere. Running and playing until they saw the approaching strangers. A wagon with a young couple came out to meet them. Libby was fourteen, and the girl on the wagon was probably younger. Yet, the girl on the wagon was heavy with child.

A man in a black suit approached. "WELCOME!" he greeted.

"My name's Brother Marsh, and you are very welcome here."

As the group headed toward the inn, most of the residents turned out. They all seemed warm and friendly in their greeting. Many of the townspeople came around the man and woman for a better look at them. It was as these strangers closed in that Libby shyly backed behind the gunman. She was frightened, and Chris Daniels knew it. Then a loud harse voice boomed, "Get back! Clear the way!"

The crowd parted quickly. There in front of these two travelers stood Deacon Zebadiah. A man in his fifties. He was just slightly taller than Libby. He had a poxmarked face, and was very short and harsh with his word. Daniels disliked him immediately.

"Take the woman into the inn," he ordered the women standing nearby.

"Sir, what's your business here?" asked the deacon. Before Daniels could speak, the deacon yelled at the others still standing there.

"You women got chores to tend to!" He ordered. "Git at 'em!" Obediently they followed their orders.

"Well, sir, what is your businesss?" again asked the deacon.

It was then that Daniels explained about the wagon train. The news upset both Brother Marsh and Deacon Zebadiah. "So she's the one that was brought here to be my bride," said the deacon. "These young ones are usually more trouble than their worth," stated the deacon rather matter of factly.

The deacon did not notice the sudden squint in the gunman's eyes, nor could he detect the flames that flared in the tall man's soul. "I got to git me some supplies," snapped Daniels.

"Yes, yes," said Brother Marsh. "The shopkeeper will be glad to tend to your needs."

"Good, sooner I'm on my way the better," said Daniels.

In the general store he filled both saddlebags, and a double pack for the draft horse. As he prepared to leave he heard footstep running toward him. He did not turn around. "You leaving?" asked the familiar voice he'd grown accustomed to.

"Yep!" He answered.

"You weren't even going to say good-bye," she accused. Daniels was silent and did not turn around. Quietly she backed away from Christian Daniels, as tears began to run down her cheeks.

The gunman stepped in the stirrup and swung up into the

saddle. As he tucked his hat to keep the sun from his eyes, he saw Libby standing there. Angrily he raked the grullo with his spurs. The startled horse jumped and bolted away, with the draft horse in tow. The tears still flowed down her cheeks as she watched her only friend disappear.

Shortly, several of the women came to her and took her to the Marsh's for lunch. The women talked until it was time for the supper meals to be prepared.

"We are all looking forward to your wedding," said Mrs. Marsh. The girl smiled, an unfeeling gesture. "You can wear my dress, if you'd like," continued Mrs. Marsh. "When we finish supper, I'll fit the dress so it'll be ready for your wedding tomorrow," said Mrs. Marsh.

"Tomorrow?" questioned Libby in a stunned tone.

"Yes, Deacon Zebadiah arranged the ceremony for tomorrow noon," stated Brother Marsh's wife.

"I...I don't even know him." began Libby.

"You will, deary, you will," said Mrs. Marsh with a knowing smile.

Mrs. Marsh lent Libby a dress for the supper meal.

"I've invited Deacon Zebadiah to supper," announced Brother Marsh when he arrived home for the evening meal.

The Deacon arrived shortly and Libby was introduced to him by Brother Marsh. Brother Marsh went inside the house and left the two people on the porch.

Libby was frightened, embarrassed, and nervous. The Deacon and his bride-to-be sat on the porch swing. Libby blushed a purplish-red as the man reached over and took her hand.

"Can you cook?" asked the church elder without concern.

"Y...Yes, sir," answered the girl meekly.

He pulled her hand as though he was helping her from the swing. She stood up.

"Now," he ordered, "let me see you, turn around."

"No," blushed Libby totally embarrassed by his stare. He was looking her over like a man buying a horse. Without warning, he slapped her across the face with the back of his hand.

"Don't ever tell me NO!" he roared.

The girl trembled still caught in his grip. "Now turn around!" He ordered again.

Holding her mouth, she obeyed.

Mr. Marsh came to the door and called them to supper.

Libby could not eat, and asked to be excused. She went to the room the Marshes had let her use tonight. It was dusk outside, but she did not light her lamp.

Mrs. Marsh had provided, her, with a nightgown to sleep in. After dressing for bed, she sat by the window and watched the draft horse in the adjoining meadow graze. Her tears seemed endless. Feeling totally helpless and alone she went to bed.

It was a long time before she fell asleep. By the time sleep came, she knew what her future held. She knew she would have a painful future, with hard work and no frills. This man she was marrying would never be a friend, just the father of her children and the ruler of her life.

Sometime before dawn she was rudely awakened by rough hands.

"Git up!" whispered a commanding voice. A hand slipped over her mouth. "Angel, it's me!" said the figure hiddened by darkness.

The girl recognized the voice. It brought her fully awake in a hurry.

The voice spoke again. "Com' on git these on," he said as clothes were pushed into her hand. He removed his hand from her mouth and turned around so she could get dressed. Hurriedly, she pulled on the trousers and shirt he'd brought.

Darkness prevented her from seeing the man distinctly. Stuffing the tail of the shirt into her trousers, she could sense the urgency in her companion. Silently, a hand reached out and grasped the back of her shirt collar. She was pulled to the open window.

Exiting first, the man then reached in the window and pulled her out. His hand closed tightly over her wrist as he ran toward the bridled draft horse. "That is our horse!" said the girl, surprised that the horse she had watched grazing was their draft horse.

Reaching the draft horse he grasped reins and mane, and swung up on the broad bare back of the huge black horse. Reaching down, he grabbed her arm and pulled the willing girl up behind him. The heavy horse moved quickly and quietly through the meadow.

Leaving the field through the gate at the back of the field, the grullo was found there waiting for them. In total silence the man dismounted the draft horse and swung up into the mustang's saddle. The pair pointed their horses into the darkness and headed away from town.

The sun had just begun to show on the horizon, and the dew was falling when they pulled up their horses by a clump of trees. The grass was very wet after the heavy dew.

Daniels pulled his slicker from his bedroll and put it on the ground for them to sit on.

The girl prepared breakfast, in the morning silence. Neither man, nor girl had spoken.

After eating, Chris finally spoke, "Guess your wondering what I'm doing."

She glanced up from blowing the steam from her coffee cup and said nothing, but her smile spoke for her. He then continued, "I couldn't leave you there. Don't ask me why, but I couldn't."

"I was to be married today..." began Libby.

Almost angrily Daniels snapped, "He'll have to live without you!" You ain't marrying nobody today, nor anytime soon."

Libby said nothing. She was just thankful that he had come for her when he did. "I got a friend, Jake Karcher. He's got a place down in the breaks. I'm taking you there now," he said. "Lessen, you want to go elsewhere," he added.

She surprised him with her answer. "Anywhere's fine with me," she began. "Just so long as it ain't back there."

Chris Daniels knew her words meant more than they actually said. He glanced at her, but she said no more. He knew something had happened, but he did not ask questions. He had hoped she would be glad to leave, but there was something...

Whatever, at this moment he knew he'd done the right thing in snatching her away from her husband-to-be. Not that that made any difference to him.

He had grown use to her and hell, she needed him, he had told himself.

As he brushed the horses, Libby readied the packs. The mustang was full of himself—especially since he didn't have to be on good behavior for the girl's safety. Libby was on the draft horse, so he took this opportunity to show his stuff. He reared, bucked, sunfished, jumped and twisted all in the same move, then landed stiff-legged.

The gunman fought the ornery grullo's every move. Chris pulled the fighting mustang up. Then spoke to the girl, "Let's head out of here. Sooner we get moving the sooner we'll get there."

Late in the afternoon, the terrain changed. The trail became dangerously rough. Finally, it became necessary for the riders to dismount and lead their horses until time to make camp. As they walked the girl found her tongue and talked like never before.

Chris found himself telling her things about his earlier life that he hadn't thought about in years. She listened intently, never prying or asking too many questions.

Early the next morning they continued their trip. Due to the extremely rough terrain, they had to lead their horses again. Several times during the day Daniels had the girl step into the grullo's saddle as he led the horses. The terrain grew rougher and steeper. Much of the trail was blocked by fallen rocks and huge boulders.

Then as if not dangerous enough, the trail narrowed, It was tricky and slow going on this stretch.

Night had fallen before they reached a campsite. The gunman spent a lot of time putting salve on the bruises and scrapes the horses had substained.

Libby was tired, but cooked a good hot supper. She then cleaned up the plates and readied the packs before turning in. Sleep came quickly to the travelers. She slept late in the morning and the gunman let her sleep. It was mid-morning before she awoke.

"Good morning, sleepy-head," greeted Chris. "I thought you was dead there for a spell." He laughed, at his joke.

"Why didn't you wake me?" she asked. "I didn't aim to slow you down."

He smiled, "I figured the horses could use the rest, and besides, you needed to make up some of that sleep you missed."

Once again they traveled till sun down.

* * * * *

The next morning she was up before sunrise. She strolled down to the creek and bathed while Chris saddled the little range horse and bridled the draft horse.

There were several head of buffalo grazing on the far side of the creek, two elk walked slowly through the eating herd. One large, olive-green bull frog sat on a dead tree stump at the edge of the stream. The hum of mosquitos could be heard before they were seen. Libby did not stay at the water long.

On her way back to camp she stopped long enough to pick some pretty wildflowers. Chris sat patiently by the campfire waiting for her to return. She smiled when she saw him. He returned her grin.

"Com' on, slow poke," he urged.

They crossed a small mountain range. It soon was obvious that this was familiar territory to the gunman. They saw several buzzards circling high in the sky. A cougar growled in the distance as the afternoon sun beat down.

The grass was mixed with heavy brush along this part of the trail. Most of this brush was full of thorns, making travel painful to both horses and their riders. Clearing the brush, they spotted a bear stealing honey from bees in an old decaying tree.

There was a sharp curve of the trail, then suddenly it widened into an improved road. The road was heavily packed dirt and wide enough for a wagon. Once upon the easier traveling road, the horses quickened their pace.

The road wound around clumps of trees, a lake and several huge boulders. Daniels turned to point out something to the girl. What had appeared as a spot in the distance, soon grew into a ranch. There was a ranchhouse, several barns and numberous outbuildings.

The huge ranchhouse was a yellowing-white with a tile roof. There were roses growing on a busted trellis in the center of the front veranda. Shortly, the two travelers pulled their horses up at the hitch rail.

A big burly man came from the ranch house. He carried a .50 caliber buffalo gun in a businesslike manner. The huge man squinted at the two horsemen. "HELL FIRE!" called out his booming voice. "The dead have risen! Christian Daniels is here!" he continued.

"Howdy, Jake, you old Indian scalper! How ya been?" fondly greeted the gunman.

"Git off'n that nag and drag that rotten ass of yourn in here!" ordered the rancher.

Daniels swung down, out of his saddle as the rancher went into the house. He reached up to help the girl off the Percheron's back, but she pushed his hands away. The loud boisterous manner of the rancher had frightened her.

Showing the tenderness and understanding that was reserved for Libby, alone, he talked to her. "Have I asked you to do anything that would hurt you?" he asked.

Her blue eyes had the frightened doe look that he had grown to hate. He did not blame the girl. It was that damn Willie Coulter's fault, and it was Willie Coulter who would pay for it one day. Not waiting for her to answer he reached up and lifted her off the horse.

She did not resist. As he released his grip of her waist, after she was standing on the ground, he smiled at her. A wisp of a smile crossed her lips, then faded quickly.

"Angel, you wait here. I'm going to talk to Jake."

She did not answer, but nodded she would wait.

Chris Daniels entered the house. Jake was please to see his friend, "Where's the girl?"

"Outside, she's a might skittish," answered Daniels.

"Powerful young for you," stated the rancher.

"That's what I wanted to talk to you about," began the gunman. "I found her, more dead than alive, a while back." Then he explained, "Our old friend, Willie Coulter, done his damnest to kill her," spoke Chris angrily.

The mere mention of Coulter's name brougt the veins out on the rancher's neck. "That son of a bitch, up to his old tricks again, huh?" asked the rancher, through gritted teeth. "What happened to the girl?"

"She was on a wagon train. Coulter and his band of cutthroats killed everybody, but the girl. Coulter tortured the wagon master beyond recognition. Woulda' killed the girl, too, if'n he'd known she wasn't killed when the wagon fell on her. They had cut her just below the ribs," finished Daniels with a slow burning anger. He remembered the scene at the campsite too well.

The rancher shook his head. "You shoulda' killed that son of a bitch Coulter when you had the chance!"

"That's for damn sure!" agreed the gunman with strong feeling.

Changing the subject, Jake said, "Well, man, don't leave that child outside. Bring her in!"

Christian Daniels obeyed without argument. He went outside and smiling took her hand in his and led her inside.

The huge room appeared lived in. The floors were covered by dirty cow-hide rugs. An enormous fireplace with mantle caught her eye as she entered. There was a handful of books on a shelf on the wall. One wall was full of rifles, shotguns and handguns. They all appeared clean and in good working condition A bone-handled Bowie knife was stuck hilt deep in a solid oak table by the fireplace. There were brightly colored Indian blankets hanging from the other walls. Several sooted candles and holders sat around the room.

The young girl sat quietly in a chair as the two men talked. She watched them as they argued over the correct means to reach an end to their problem.

Christian Daniels was not as tall as the rancher. The rancher was probably close to six feet and a half tall, where the younger man was just an inch over six feet. Jake was built like an ox. He had huge arms, wide shoulders and enormous hands. His head looked shaggy with the long brownish-red hair that went to his shoulder. Jake had green-gray eyes and a thick handle-bar mustache.

Daniels eyes were dark like his hair. Chris was usually clean-shaven, but today he wore a two day stubble of whiskers. The gunman was strong, yet he lacked the bulging muscles of his friend.

As the two men continued to talk, Jake suddenly shouted, "Lord man!" The rancher's loud voice, boomed, "That youngin probably" bout to starve! We'll talk later."

Christian Daniels turned and smiled at the girl, as the rancher hurried off toward his kitchen. "Angel, I'm gonna put the horses up. You wait here."

"Chris..." began the girl. That frightened doe look returned to her eyes.

As Christian Daniels walked out of the house, he thought back to the time that Willie and he had worked here at the ranch. There for a time he had considered Willie a friend.

It wasn't until that day, two years ago, that he had found out just how bad Coulter was. Jake and his wife Clara had hired a group of men as they returned from the war. Coutler and Daniels were two of them. They were the youngest of the hired hands and Clara had just about adopted the pair as sons she'd never had.

Jake had always treated them more like a father than a boss.

There had been many times that Jake and Clara had had them to the house for meals.

Coulter and another hired hand had an argument about the battle of Bull Run. They got in a fight over it and Coulter just went crazy. He nearly beat the other man to death with his fist.

Finally Jake got there and pulled Coulter off the other man. He told Coulter to cool off and with the help of a cook, named Herb, helped the injured man toward the bunk house. Clara came out carrying a towel and a basin of water.

Suddenly, and without warning Coulter came from nowhere. He had a gun in each hand, and started pulling the triggers. He shot Clara first, then each of the three men in front of him.

Chris rode up just as the shooting stopped. He'd raised his rifle and drew a bead on Coulter. He recognized Willie and lowered his rifle. As Daniels ran to Clara, Coulter escaped.

Jake had been shot in the shoulder, while Herb was hit in the leg. Clara and the ranch hand were both dead.

Chris helped Jake and Herb into the bunk house. Then he buried Clara and started hunting Coulter. He had lost Coulter's trail the next day and hadn't ran into him since. He'd heard plenty about Willie's exploits though.

Daniels led the two horses to the barn, as his thoughts returned to the present.

Inside the house, Jake came down the hallway from the kitchen. The girl eyed him carefully.

Sensing her fear, he spoke, "Whoa, honey!" "Don't let this old ground-hog spook ya!" he said.

The girl said nothing, but continued to watch him. "You'll have 'th 'cuse me. I ain' been round no wimen, since my Clara was kilt."

Libby gathered her courage and spoke. "Has your wife been dead long?"

Jake thought of his Clara then. He had loved her very much. It's been two years since...since Coulter murdered her," said the rancher, trying to withhold his anger.

The girl was startled at the news. "Your wife was killed by Brother William?" she asked. The rancher nodded. The girl noticed the veins in his neck stand out.

"I'm sorry," she said earnestly.

Jake looked at the girl. He now understood what had changed

his wild, rough friend. "Young'un, when you want, you tell me 'bout gittin' that wild man to help ya!"

"Mr. Jake, sir," began the girl. "I had nothing to do with it. If'n it weren't for him I'd be dead now."

"Well, honey, you've done somethin' to that ornery devil, cause the Christian Daniels that brung ya here t'ain't the gunman I'd knowd."

The girl didn't understand. The rancher laughed, "Com'on girl, I got ya some vittles on." The girl didn't really understand why, but she found herself beginning to like this burly giant.

It was a short time later that Daniels entered the kitchen, carrying his saddle.

"Gawd Jake! Ain't you ever done no dishes!" shouted the younger man seeing the kitchen. There were dirty pots and skillets everywhere. Dirty tin plates were stacked on the floor, pantry and on the table.

Daniels went to his pack and took out his plate. He heaped it full of food from the pots on the stove.

The girl began clearing the table as soon as she finished eating. She left Daniels' plate while he finished. She heated water and was busy scraping the old dirty plates when Daniels brought her his plate.

He sat on the cabinet and talked to the girl as she worked at this task. "Well, how do you like it here?" he asked.

"It's...it's nice," she said.

"Jake still scare you?" he asked.

"Sometimes," she answered truthfully. Then turning she smiled at her friend, "but you know what, I think I'm gonna like him."

This brought a grin to the face of her friend. She noted his warm friendly smile. His eyes shined and she knew she was extremely lucky that he had found her.

Jake and Daniels went to the large living room. "I got something...I gotta ask you," stated the younger man. "Can you put me and the girl up for a spell?" At least till I can find someplace to send her," asked Daniels.

"Can I!?!" asked the rancher. "You just try taking out of here with that youn'un in tow."

Daniels laughed. "You got someplace the kid can sleep tonite?" he asked.

"Of course! I done put Clara's good bed clothes on the bed in the back while supper was cooking."

"And now Christian Daniels if you'll haul that lazy ass of your'n out back you can tote in Clara's tub. That youn'un probaably wantin' to wash," stated Jake.

"Yes, siree," mockingly answered the younger man.

"GAWD DAMN!" echoed the gunman's voice from the kitchen. The rancher hurried to the kitchen. He was dumbfounded. Libby had cleaned not only the supper dishes, but all the other dirty plates, pots and skillets. She had cleared the stove, pantry and the table. It was a different place.

Jake stood at the door and finally spoke. "This reminds me of when Clara was here." It was apparent that the rancher was overcome with emotion. Libby looked up and Chris winked at her, and nodded an approving glance.

In less than an hour, the men had heated enough water to fill the tub. As the girl bathed in the kitchen, the men sat in the front room and smoked some stogies Jake had saved for a special occasion.

After several puffs, Daniels said to his friend, "Gawd Jake, how can you smoke these things?" he held the green-cured smoke away from his face.

"Aw hell, Chris, this separates the men from the boys, 'side they'll grow on ya," laughed the rancher. "Just like shoveling shit the first time, enough to gag a maggot. After a spell, hell, you don't think no more about it than taking a piss," he concluded.

"Jake, where the hell is everybody? I ain't seen a hired hand, since I got here."

"I ain't got none. I let 'em all go," said Jake. "With Clara dead, the ranch didn't mean much to me no more."

"That's a helluva note, Jake! After you carved this place outa the wilderness. You fought the Comanches, the Apach', the weather and squatters; and now you just sit back and let it all go to rot! Jake, what the hell were you thinking of?" angrily asked the younger man.

"That's 'bout the size of it, I drank and remembered, then drank more to forgit," confessed the older man.

Chris kicked back his chair.

"Where the hell ya goin'?" asked the rancher.

"I gotta check on the girl," he said as he left the room.

"You know, I wish the hell Clara was here. She never would believe what I just heard!"

Before entering the kitchen, Chris turned and faced the older man. "Oh, shut up! You old buzzard." Yet, he could feel color come to his face, and he knew he couldn't hide his feelings for the girl from the rancher. Even the urge to stand there and argue with the rancher, didn't stop Chris Daniels from going on and checking on Libby.

The girl was out of the tub, and apparently in the extra room. Gently he knocked on the door. There was no answer.

Quietly he opened the door. The girl was asleep in the big feather bed. As though stalking game, he moved noiselessly across the room, and blew out her lamp. Before leaving he pulled her blanket up and tucked it in.

She was sleeping so peacefully that it was hard to recognize the pain-riddled face of the girl he had found. Leaving the room, he saw Jake standing there.

"Everything allright?" asked the rancher with concern.

The gunman nodded. The two men returned to the front room.

"She scared the hell out of me those first few days after I found her," began Daniels. "There were so many times that I thought I'd lost her. Then when I got her to King's Fork..." here he hesitated. "That damn old bastard...he had 'em buy him a young bride."

Here Jake tried to relieve the anger in his friend. "Well you wouldn't buy an old bride?" laughed the rancher.

Daniels looked at the rancher with those soul-piercing dark eyes, without a smile or comment. Perhaps, if it was anyone but the girl, Daniels might have laughed too.

Jake realized then, just how much his young hot-headed friend cared for the young woman.

Then, in one of the few occasions that Jake could remember, Christian Daniels spoke with emotion, "I couldn't leave her for that bastard!" confessed Daniels. "She didn't belong with those people."

It was here that Jake spoke up. "Well, she's welcome here for as long as she wants."

Daniels knew the rancher meant what he'd said. "Thank you, my friend," said the young gunman.

Jake and Chris dumped the water from the tub. "One of these

days, I'll try out this tub," laughed Jake.

Daniels agreed, "It sure couldn't hurt!"

The younger man picked up his saddle and tack which was by thing the back door. "Chris, you can bunk out on the sofa in the other room. It's good bedding, when Clara was upset, I spent several nights on it."

"Thanks, Jake, but I'll sleep here," stated the gunman.

Jake watched as the younger man shook out his bedroll in the hallway between the kitchen and the extra room. The rancher put the candles out in the front room before going to the main bedroom in the front of the house.

As he pulled his boots off on the bootjack, he looked at the tin-type of him and his beloved Clara. "Well, darlin', Chris done got himself mixed-up in someptin' he can't run from." He paused an instant. "You was right, too. I'da never believed it, but under that wild, hell-bent-for-leather hide there's a down right decent man there!"

"Now, Clara, you ain't gonna believe this neither, but if'n I'm any judge of wimmen that youn'un he fetched in'll make his hair turn gray!" With this thought, Jake laughed, a hearty enjoyable chuckle. Then he blew out the lamp and turned in.

Both men were awakened by the aroma of brewed coffee and fried bacon. The girl had also fixed fried potatoes and scrambled some eggs.

"Lordy!" Shouted Jake entering the kitchen. "I done died and went to heaven!"

Libby laughed and piled the food on his plate. Daniels came in the back door. He had gone to the pump to wash up for breakfast.

"Morn'in Jake," greeted the younger man.

Ignoring the younger man's greeting Jake looked at his plate, then at the girl. "Good Lord girl, do you have any idea at'all how long it's been since I hadda meal like this'in?"

Libby just laughed as she used the apron she had on to pull a pan of biscuits out of the oven. Jake wasted no more time talking, he was busy shoveling in the food.

Wiping her hands on the apron, she sat down in a chair Daniels had shoved out for her with his foot.

Both men were still eating when she finished. Again she started cleaning up. As the men finished she washed their plates too.

"Mr. Jake..." began the girl.

"Honey, you call me Jake, okay?" said the rancher.

"Yes, sir," she answered. "Do you have a broom?"

"Nope, but you give me a spell and I'll make one," he answered.

Libby went outside. A short time later she came in carrying a large pan of water for the stove. Chris Daniels stopped her at the door. "What do you think your doin'?" Before she could answer he continued, "You need anything," he said, "you tell me."

"Or me!" Yelled Jake.

"Chris, would you mind fetchin' in the tub again?" asked the girl.

Chris nodded and yelled, "Jake, haul your ass out here."

The two men went outside to bring the tub back in.

"She ain't gonna bath-again, is she?" Asked the rancher.

"Now how the hell do I know?" Answered the younger man.

Together they carried in the heavy iron tub. Libby thanked them, then looked like she was going to ask something, but changed her mind.

"What?" asked Daniels to her unasked question.

"Would you mind bringing in some water for the tub?" She asked hesitantly.

As the two men carried in buckets of water, Chris spoke. "I guess that answers your question."

They put most of the water they carried into kettles on the stove. After they filled all the kettles, they looked for Libby, but she had disappeared.

Shortly, Libby emerged from the room Jake had provided for her to sleep in. She was carrying the curtains from that room, and also the clothes from her bed. "Chris, Jake, if'n you'll bring me your clothes, I'll git 'em washed for you."

"Whoa, honey," began the rancher, "you got no business doin' man's wash."

Libby smiled, "I've done my Grandpap's longhandles for years."

A rather shocked rancher looked to his friend for assistance. "I can't take no fee-male hee-hawing at my longjohns!"

He found no sympathy from his friend. The younger man was too busy laughing.

"Go ahead and bray like a Jackass!" gripped the rancher. "Wait'll she washes your drawers!"

"Jake...sir..." began the girl. "Do you have any soap made?"

"'Course. What do you think I am? A heathen or somepthin'?" he asked angrily as Daniels laughed.

Jake went to the cupboard and got out a hunk of soap. He tried blowing the dust off it, then finally tried wiping it off with his shirt tail. When that failed, he tossed it in the tub of hot water.

"Thank ya," said the girl, as the men dumped their clothes in the tub.

She heard some hammering out back. Wiping her soapy hands on the apron, she looked out the window. Jake and Chris were running a rope across the backyard for a clothes line.

* * * * *

By noontime all the clothes were hanging on the line.

Libby called the men for lunch. She had cooked up some beans, and made some corn sticks. Both men ate all they could hold.

Soon after lunch, Jake came in carrying the broom he had been working on. When Libby called the two men for supper, they found a different house.

There was still a lot of cleaning to do, but you could notice the change on entry. This brought a frown to Daniels' face.

"I didn't bring you here to be no servant girl!" he stated angrily.

"I know," she answered.

"Lord knows this place needs a woman's touch." began the rancher. "But you let me take care of it. There's a widow in Pleasant that I hear'd needed work. I'll fetch her out here to care for the place."

"Chris...Jake...I don't mind carrying for the house," stated the girl. "I did it for years for Grandpap." she continued.

Sh..h..h," said Daniels. "Jake's got the right idea."

Libby had fixed fried cured ham and boiled potatoes for their supper. As the men ate, they decided they'd go to town first light of the morning.

While the men finished eating, Libby went outside and took down her wash. When she came back in Chris spoke, "We'll be goin' to Pleasant tomorrow. You make a list of things you'll need when we git to town."

"Will I need to wear these 'boy's clothes' to town?" she asked hesitantly.

Looking rather regretfully Chris spoke, "I'm afraid so," he

began. "I pitched those other clothes that I'd picked up at the wagon train," he said.

"Oh..h.," she said, the disappointment showing on her face.

As she went to her room Daniels sat back in his chair. Without warning he pulled the hunting knife from its sheath on his thigh and threw it at the wall. The heavy knife buried its blade into the wall as the walnut handle quivered.

"I feel like that myself, sometimes," commented the rancher rather matter of factly.

"She gets all fretted up 'bout wearing trousers 'round folks. 'Fraid they'll think evil of her," stated the gunman.

"No decent folks would think thatta way, 'specially if'n they knew what'd happened," said Jake.

"Me'n you know that, but try telling the little one," said the younger man.

The men turned in for the night.

When Libby got up to fix breakfast, she was surprised. There on the table was a calico dress.

Chris Daniels was awakened by Libby kissing his forehead.

"Thank you, oh,...thank you." She hugged his neck.

He had never been so pleasantly awakened before. At first he thought he had been dreaming. Libby hurried off into her room. She returned shortly, and began preparing breakfast. She found some sugar and made syrup, then fixed flapjacks.

"Thank you, Mr. Karcher," said the girl when Jake came to breakfast. The burly rancher with his heavy morning whiskers growth blushed.

"Clara woulda made two of ya, easy; but she woulda been sore if'n I didn't see ya was dressed proper. Bein' dressed proper was 'portant to Clara."

Libby was too excited to eat. She waited impatiently for the men to finish eating. She was surprised, when Daniels looked at her and said, "You go head and get ready for town."

"Me and Jake'll wash the dishes this morning," said the younger man.

Libby hesitated, but Chris looked at her with those dark brown eyes and moved his head toward to door. "Go on, git!"

The two men finished their meal, then the dishes and finally hitched up the wagon and still no sign of the girl. "Libby!" called Daniels. "Libby, you goin'?"

There was no response. "L I B B Y!!! yelled Daniels again.

"I'm coming," answered the girl. Running out the door, she was dressed all in calico. She had doubled the waist up with a belt.

"Well, young lady, don't you look purty!" exclaimed Jake. She blushed, but she was proud of how she looked. Her blonde hair was pulled back and her blue eyes sparkled.

Christian Daniels lifted her up onto the buckboard. She sat next to Jake, while Daniels swung up on the grullo. The little mustang pitched a fit. With one mighty buck he sent Daniels sprawling on the ground, knocking the wind out of him.

Libby started to jump down from the buckboard, but Jake grabbed her arm.

As soon as he realized his rider was missing, the little horse stopped. The grullo tossed his head, throwing his long black mane to one side. Seeing his rider lying on the ground he lowered his head and walked to him. Nudging the prone rider, he whinnied softly.

The air came back to the gunman's lungs shortly. Stunned, he sat up. The little horse stood quietly beside his master.

"Are you allright?" asked Jake.

"Yea, I think so," answered the younger man.

"Now, look what you've done!" scolded the horseman to the horse.

When Daniels got to his feet the horse stood quietly. This time when he swung into the saddle he had a different reception. The horse was almost too gentle. Cautiously, he picked each step. Daniels snapped up the reins and set the horse after the buckboard.

The gunman had to grin to himself as he watched the girl try and keep her dress from blowing.

The trail narrowed, between walls of rocks on this stretch. A small puma cub stood on a rock ledge and growled at the travelers. Clearing the rocks, the road widened and the ground was level.

Nearly and hour later, they reached the town called Pleasant. It was a small frontier town. A general store, a livery, a bank and two saloons.

"You two go on to the general store," said Jake. "I'm gonna find the Widow Jackson."

Daniels grinned as he watched Jake hurry across the street toward the Lucky Dollar Saloon. Chris knew the Widow Jackson would not be found in there.

Chris turned and helped Libby off the buckboard. They entered the store and began finding the supplies they needed. Libby was looking at cloth on the far side of the store when Chris heard a hissing sound behind him. He turned and saw Jake motioning for him to come outside. "Com' here, Chris!" urged the rancher.

Daniels could detect the urgency in the rancher's tone. Outside the two men walked to the other side of the buckboard.

"All hell's done busted loose!" spoke the rancher obviously upset.

"What?" questioned the gunman.

The burly rancher reached out and grabbed the younger man by the shoulders. "There's been a massacre!" King's Fork's been burned to the ground!"

The news took the younger man by surprise. "Damn it, Willie Coulter is murdering again!" Shouted the rancher angrily.

Daniels nodded. The blood in his veins turned cold as he thought, "My God! If I hadn't gone back for 'Angel'..." He left his thought unfinished.

Suddenly he snapped, "For God's sake don't say nothing to the kid about this!"

"Your damn right, I won't!" agreed the older man.

When they looked around, Libby stood at the store's window. Both men entered the store. Supplies were bought, the buckboard loaded and the Widow Jackson found.

The widow was pleased with the job offer, and accepted it immediately. The widow had always thought Jake Karcher a good looking gentleman in the rough.

Jake helped the widow and Libby up on the buckboard for their trip home.

Christian Daniels had his hands full with the little mustang. He pulled the grullo up. Stepping out of the saddle, he threw the stirrup over the horn, as he tightened the cinch. Then as he watched the wagon disappear up the trail, he adjusted the tough grullo's bridle. Before catching up to the buckboard, he watered his horse.

He laughed as the mustang took his hoof, and sent a school of minnows swimming. When the horse had finished drinking, Daniels lowered the stirrup and swung into the saddle. The fiesty little horse was ready to run, and his rider did not stop him.

As the small front hooves reached out, the shiny gray horse with the dark line down his back and the black mane and tail literally flew. In just a few moments, the pair caught up with the slow moving wagon.

Libby turned and looked back as the pair came closer. One glance at the girl and Daniels realized she had found out about King's Fork. There's was no mistaking the "frightened doe" look in those dark blue eyes.

"Damn Jake, and his big mouth!" thought the horseman.

Quickly Daniels urged the horse up beside the wagon. "Pull up Jake!" shouted the horseman. The wagon rumbled to a stop.

"Whatt's matter?" questioned the driver.

Christian Daniels ignored the rancher's question. "Honey," began the horseman. "Com'on" he said, as he reached up to her.

While she moved around the Widow Jackson, Daniels moved his foot out of the stirrup. Then the girl stepped into the stirrup, and with Daniel's help she swung up behind him.

The mustang tossed his head throwing his heavy mane in the air. The group began moving again.

"Have you heard?" she asked.

Knowing what she meant, he nodded "yes." "Angel, don't you fret about it..."

Hesitantly, she asked, "...was...was it, was it like the wagon train?"

"I don't know, Angel...I 'mgine it 'twas," he answered honestly.

She sat silently for a long time. Finally she asked, "Why?"

"Money, probably," began Daniels." "Money, power, and just plain crazy."

"Chris, I'm scared," she confessed.

"I know...I know you are," he agreed with compassion.

The ranch house came into view, and it was good to be home.

Jake helped the widow off the buckboard. He then started unloading the wagon. Daniels slid off his horse, then helped Libby off the horse. Rather than tend to the horses first, Daniels took Libby into the house.

Jake and the widow watched as the gunman walked slowly with the girl into the house. It was apparent to them that Christian Daniels was very concerned about the girl. He had a ready smile and gentle words for her every statement.

Mrs. Jackson came into the house and Libby began showing her the rooms. All seemed well, so Daniels went out to care for the horses, and help Jake unload the wagon.

Jake was waiting beside the buckboard with a rather puzzled look on his face. "Tell me," he said, "how'n the hell did ya know?"

"Eyes!" he answered rather sheepishly. "I know that frightened me look in her eyes."

"Reading eyes, now, huh!" grinned Jake."

Daniels nodded and grinned too. "Jake!" called out the younger man, as the other man headed for the house.

"Yeah?" answered the rancher.

"Where you gonna bed the widow down at?" asked Daniels.

"Damn if I know." said Jake scratching his chin.

It was almost two hours later before the chores were completed. The women had a hot meal awaiting them.

Daniels was eating heartily, when he noticed Libby hadn't taken a bite. "Not hungry?" he asked.

Shaking her head no, she got up from the table.

"Dearie, are you sick?" asked the widow.

"No," she answered meekly. "I guess I'm just tired." The young lady got up from the table and walked outside. Daniels said nothing, but did not remove his eyes from her.

Mrs. Jackson, a big sturdy woman, whose dark hair was streaked with gray strands, did not completely understand the situation. She was the one who had started talking of the King's Fork massacre.

Daniels waited awhile and when the girl did not come in, he went out. At first he didn't see her. Then he spotted her placing some wildflowers on Clara's grave.

He rolled himself a smoke, but flicked it away without lighting it. In the distance, he saw several horsemen. They seemed to be just riding by. Daniels was suspicious. "Libby," he called out. "Come here, girl."

The girl looked up and walked toward him without question. "Go in the house," he began. "Tell Jake to grab his scatter gun and come a runnin'!"

The young woman obeyed without hesitation. Jake wasted no time in grabbing the gun. Turning as he went out the back door he said, "You ladies stay in here!"

Daniels was already saddling the horses. The grullo sensed the urgency and stood quietly. "Might be nothin'," said the younger man, "but I'm concerned 'bout 'em. Jake," continued the younger man, "you still got that cellar where Clara use to store her preserves?"

"Sure do, but ain't been in there since Clara died."

"Best put the womenfolk in there. I sure ain't fond of the idea of riding off leaving them here alone with Willie Coulter in these parts."

The rancher looked almost shocked, "Damn, son, you don't think that bastard Coulter would come back here?"

"I...I don't know," answered the younger man earnestly.

"I'll take the ladies to the cellar."

Hiding the two women in the dark, mildewed, cob-webbed cellar, Jake hurried back to the barn. Chris was already heading the mustang in the direction he had seen the horsemen riding off in. Jake caught up in just a few strides.

Libby sat there in the dark, fighting back tears, with her chin resting on her knees. Mrs. Jackson nervously rung her hands.

The girl saw the older woman's distress, and went over to comfort her. She forgot her own fear as she helped the other lady. "Don't you fret none. Mr. Daniels won' let 'em hurt us," she assured.

"But if it's Coulter's bunch...you just don't know what they could do..." said Mrs. Jackson.

The girl smiled. "Your wrong there ma'am."

Then Libby explained how Christian Daniels had found her. Maybell Jackson sat there spellbound, as she listened to the story. When she heard the facts she too forgot her fear.

Before Libby finished the tale, Daniels had returned and opened the cellar door. Reaching in, he grasped Mrs. Jackson's hand and helped her out of the cellar. Then he reached in and helped the girl out. "You okay?" he asked.

"Yes, it wasn't too bad," she confessed. "But, I was scared." Daniels gave her that reassuring smile, that she had seen so much in the past.

"Is everything alright?" asked the widow.

"Jake's following 'em for a spell, but it just looked like ranchhands to me," answered the man.

The ladies returned to the kitchen as Daniels cleaned his rifle, then the six-gun.

Several hours past, but Jake did not return. Daniels began pacing the floor, like a puma on the prowl. As darkness fell, there was still no sign of Jake.

"Damn his ass!" growled the younger man. "I shoulda hauled his mangy hide back with me!"

The women were just finishing their evening chores when the sound of galloping hooves echoed through the night. Daniels threw the kitchen table over on its side and called the women. Mrs. Jackson quickly ducked behind the table. Libby stood there, unsure of what was going on.

Angrily, Daniels reached out and grabbed Libby by the arm and jerked her down behind the table.

A knock came at the back door. Libby caught a glimpse of steel as the gunman, holding her head down, drew his gun with the other hand.

"Mr. Daniels! Mr. Daniels!" called a young male voice.

"Who wants him?" answered Daniels.

"I'm Ben Hawkins, sir," replied the voice from beyond the door. "Mr Karcher's horse fell. He's been hurt, sir, Mr. Karcher wanted you to fetch him a wagon, sir."

"How bad he hurt?" asked the gunman, still uncertain of the truth.

"He got banged up pretty good," said the boy. "Ma says he'll be alright though. He busted his arm, and bumped his head some."

"Son, if this is some kinda trick, you won't live to see the sun come up in the mornin'," warned the gunman.

No, sir! I wouldn't lie to you, sir," answered the young man honestly.

"Ma'am," addressed the gunman to the widow. "You ever hear of this boy before?"

"Yes, his folks are squatters up in the breaks. Their farm ain't much, they're poor but honest."

"Thanks," said Christian as he nodded. He lit the lantern on the floor beside him. Righting the table, he then opened the door and asked the young fella in.

Ben Hawkins was a gangly boy. All legs and arms with little meat on his bones. He had blonde, almost white hair with eyes as blue as Libby's. His face would have been better looking if he hadn't all those pimples.

There was no doubt in the gunman's mind that Jake was in trouble. "Christian Daniels is the name," introduce the gunman.

The younger man hardly noticed Daniels. He hadn't taken his eyes off Libby since entering the room.

"Ma'am," he said to the girl.

Libby smiled at him. Her gleaming white teeth glittered in the lantern light.

"Howdy, Ben," greeted Mrs. Jackson.

He either ignored her or didn't hear her, because he addressed the younger woman. "What's your name?" he asked.

"Libby Ward," answered the girl as color came to her face.

"Libby...that's a pretty name. That's my Ma's name too."

"I'll go hitch up the team," said Daniels.

Ignoring the gunman, he asked, "Have you lived here long, Libby?"

Shaking her head she answered, "No."

Shortly Daniels called out for Ben. The boy did go to the wagon then. Christian Daniels returned to the house for his rifle.

The girl was waiting at the door. "You be careful," she said sincerely.

"I will," he said rather harshly. "And I'll take care of that love sick puppy too!" He did not wait for her response.

It was noon the next day before the men returned home. Ben's mother, Elizabeth or Libby for short, had tended to Jake's injuries. Ben's father, Otto, searched for Jake's horse.

Jake was grumpier than a grizzly bear. Nothing pleased him.

Libby went to the pump for a bucket of water. Ben eagerly ran over to do the pumping. When the bucket was full, he insisted on carrying it into the house for her.

Daniels was pitching hay from the loft of the barn, but stopped and watched the whole scene from the hayloft window.

Mrs. Jackson had prepared a meal for them when all the chores were done. As they finished their meal, Ben asked Libby to go for a walk.

Jake razzed his friend after the young couple left the table. "That young fella sure is taken by her," said the rancher.

Jake Karcher was not prepared for the angry look he received as Daniels glanced up from his meal.

Jake was not to be outdone. "Seen a man turn so green one time, 'few years back. Had to white-wash him back to his natural color." The rancher then laughed, and found his statement so humorous that he broke into a hee-hawing.

"Very funny!" snapped the gunman rudely.

"Aw, God, Chris, she's gonna be havin' fellas fallin' all over themselves. She's a fine lookin' gal. And she's gonna be one hell of a woman!"

"I know that!" snapped Christian Daniels hotly.

"I don't care how many of 'em like her, long as they don't git outa line!" warned the young lady's rescuer.

Jake realized then just how much his friend cared for the girl. He also realized that for the fella who got out to line life would be definitely painful, and probably short! The young woman's guardian angel would guarantee that.

Ben and Libby returned shortly. They were laughing and talking about things of interest to people of their age. Ben said his good-byes, then headed home for his evening chores.

Libby walked over to Daniels, who was sitting in the main room on a hide-covered chair. "Ben wants to go on a picnic Sunday," she began. "Is it okay with you if I go?"

Libby was startled by the gunman's angry reply. "Hell yes! Why ask me, I ain't your kin!"

"But..." she started.

"But, Hell! you ain't nothing to me!" roared the gunman hatefully. This stopped Libby. Quietly she turned her back to him and left the room.

"You are one hell of a bastard!" said Jake.

The morning was overcast and there was a feeling of rain in the air. Mrs. Jackson had breakfast ready at dawn. Jake was feeling better. His injuries were troubling him far less than the day before.

The rage in Daniels had ebbed too. "I guess I made an ass of myself last night," he said. To his surprise, both Mrs. Jackson and Jake agreed whole heartedly.

"Where's Libby?" asked Jake.

"Still asleep, I guess," said Mrs. Jackson. "I'll go wake her."

"That's all right," said Daniels. "I'll call her. I've got to tell her I was mean." He pushed away from the table and went to the room. He knocked softly on her door. "Libby," he said.

"Breakfast is ready."

There was no response. "We been through too much for you not to say something." Still there was no reply. "Libby!" he said, opening the door.

In the kitchen they heard his yell. "SHIT!!" he roared. That was followed by his call, "Jake! She's gone!!"

"What?" questioned the rancher in disbelief.

"My God! She's been out alone all night," exclaimed the younger man.

Daniels literally ran for the door. He quickly threw his saddle on the grullo, As he led the gray horse from the barn, he noticed the Percheron missing.

Leaning out of the saddle, almost to the gray horse's knee, he followed the big horse's tracks. The tracks were big and easy to follow. Christian, using his hat, urged the grullo from a slow lope into a full gallop. Suddenly he pulled the mustang up. The horse stopped stiff-legged in the front, sitting back on his haunches as he skidded to a stop. Gravel and rocks scattered from the hooves. There was the horse and the girl coming toward him.

"I didn't have no place to go," he said.

"Get off that horse!" he ordered. "Do you know you had me scared to death!"

"I didn't think you cared," she stated, using words that cut like a knife.

"You listen to me," he began harshely. "I don't always know the right thing to say. Sometimes...I can't say nothing right, but, you remember this, come hellfire or the devil himself, I care about you! You're the only important thing in my life," he confessed unashamed.

She wrapped her arms around him and hugged him.

"You go have your picnic," he said with a smile. "But, don't ever—and I mean EVER, run off in the middle of the night again!" She nodded. "Angel, we will disagree, we might even yell at each other, but don't ever think you have to run away."

The two friends walked their horses back to the ranch. They had just reached the ranch when they saw a rider approach. Daniels apparently knew him, as he walked over to greet him.

The breathless rider saw Daniels and said, "Daniels, the foreman sent me. We got big trouble brewing with a group of squatters. They've cut off the water with a dam. Their leader told the foreman that we'll get water over their dead bodies. You know why I'm here. Bossman said, I was to tell you he'll pay top dollar for this job."

"Tell Hank, I'll see him by the end of the week," said Daniels.

The rider smiled, "YES, sir!" Then with a flick of his reins the horse pivoted and was gone, Christian Daniels watched him ride away.

When the rider was out of sight, Daniels entered the house. "They're havin' nester trouble at the Triple Peaks spread," announced the gunman.

"You git the job?" asked Jake.

"Yea, you think you're up to taking care of things here?" asked Daniels with concern.

"I reckon," answered the rancher.

"I'l plan on leaving first light," stated the younger man rather matter of factly.

"Think you'll be gone long?" inquired Jake.

"Never know, but I'll probably be back in a couple of weeks."

"Libby," called Daniels. "Come here a minute. "Let's go for a walk," said Daniels. They walked away from the house and to the stream that ran behind the house.

"I'm going away for a spell," he began.

She was silent, and watched the water as it rippled over rocks in the stream. Christian continued, "Jake, he'll take good care of you till I get back."

With her back to him she nodded. "Can I go with you?" she asked.

"NO!" he answered firmly. "No place for a young lady in a cow camp. 'Sides you got a picnic to go to."

Again she nodded. "Promise me, Angel," said Daniels," You ain't gonna run off alone again, are you?"

She said nothing, but shook her head no. He reached out and gently placed his arm around her shoulder and they walked in silence for a long time. Finally they returned to the ranchhouse.

Libby awoke early the next morning, but her friend was already gone. She didn't eat breakfast, instead she walked outside and sat on the top rail of the corral and watched the Percheron.

Jake finished eating, then came out and walked to the girl. "Don't you be frettin' none 'bout that ole war dog. He knows how to take care of himself. And honey, if'n you think highly of 'im, you'll need to know he's doin' now what he's always done."

"Jake do you think he really will be back?"

"I figure he will, lessen' sompthin' stops him," answered the rancher.

Slowly and thoughtfully Libby walked out of the yard and up the nearby knoll where wildflowers were blooming. She picked a huge handful and brought them back with her. Walking to Clara's grave, she placed the flower in the tin cup by the marker. She was careful not to drop any of the blooms.

Jake had been busy cleaning the stalls in the barn, but stopped and leaned on the pitchfork watching the young gal and her generous gift. Libby kneeled by the marker and was pulling some tall grass away when Ben arrived.

"Hi!" said Ben, greeting Libby. Jumping off his horse, Ben asked Libby if she'd like to go over to their place. His Ma had said she'd like to meet the girl...

"I don't know..." hesitated the girl.

"Ma really wants you to come by. She really wants to meet you."

Libby was trying to decide when a voice boomed out. "Ben Hawkins!! Have you lost your manners, boy?" called out the Widow Jackson as she carried out the wash.

"No ma' am!" he answered. "How are you this morning?"

"Fine, just fine," was her reply.

"Libby, they're havin' a barn dance next Saturday. Would you go with me?" he asked nervously.

Once again she answered, "I don't know..." Libby finally answered Ben, "I'll haveta ask Jake."

"I'll ask him, if'n you'd like," offered Ben anxiously awaiting the answer.

"He's at the barn," said Libby.

Ben headed for the barn. Jake saw him coming. He reminded the rancher of a young peacock spreading his feathers.

Jake gave Ben his permission, but not before he explained to the young rooster what would happen if he didn't mind his manners.

Libby enjoyed the trip to the Hawkins place. There for a few hours she forgot how lonesome she was since her friend left. Most of the time was spent talking to Mrs. Hawkins and helping her prepare the meals. Mrs. Hawkins told Libby how nice it was to have someone there that knew how to help in the kitchen.

On the trip back to the Karcher Ranch, Ben stopped the buggy long enough to steal a kiss.

Mrs. Jackson met them at the door, and asked if they had a nice time. Libby assured her they had, but Ben decided not to come in and bid them good-night from the buggy.

* * * * *

A little after dawn the next morning Ben arrived for their picnic. He sat at the table while Jake finished his breakfast. When Jake finished, Ben went out to help him with the chores. Libby and Mrs. Jackson began frying the chicken. She had made potato salad and deviled eggs the night before.

About an hour before noon, the two young people left the ranch for their picnic. They headed for the lake on the road to town. They had decided that was an excellent place for their day.

Shortly after they left, Maybell Jackson walked out of the house, and joined Jake sitting on the porch. "Those two make such a nice couple," she commented

"Yea," answered Jake, unenthused. "I'm just damn glad Chris ain't here."

Thinking Jake was making sport of the situation she laughed and said, "Oh, go on." A stern faced Jake did not reply.

Ben and Libby enjoyed their picnic. Then Ben showed Libby how to fish. He laughed when she wouldn't hold the worm to put it on the hook. She finally caught a small sunfish, and insisted that Ben remove it from the hook. She then insisted that he release it

They were packing up their dishes when a shower caught them. Ben put the top up on the buggy, and turned his horse so the back of the buggy protected them from the rain. The young couple held up the blanket that they had used for their picnic to keep the rain from coming inside. Libby giggled as the rain began to drip in.

The rain shower stopped almost as quickly as it had begun. The heavy downpour made traveling in the buggy a slow process, as the wheels sank into the mud.

It was Jake on the porch awaiting their arrival.

"Boy, you best have a good reason for gittin' here this late," growled the burly rancher.

Before Ben could find his voice, Libby started to explain.

"Libby, go on in the house," commanded Jake. "This is man's business."

The color had left Ben's face, as he tried to explain their tardiness to the stern faced rancher.

"You realize, boy," began Jake, "You had Mrs. Jackson concerned about her safety." Then the rancher continued, "Do you want to ruin her reputation?"

Ben lost his voice, and only replied by shaking his head 'NO'.

"What would folks say? " demanded Jake. "Next time you take Libby out, you have her here at the agreed time."

Ben was relieved. Jake had not forbid him from seeing Libby. "Good night, Mr. Karcher," said Ben.

"'Night, Ben," said the rancher. "You be careful driving home in this darkness. Easy to break a wheel or an axle when you can't see."

"Yes, sir," answered Ben.

Libby was in the kitchen talking to Mrs. Jackson when Jake entered. "Jake!" called the widow. "We've gotta problem here."

"What?" exclaimed Jake.

Mrs. Jackson continued, "Libby's been invited to the barn dance."

"Sompthin' wrong with that?" asked the rancher confused.

"I don't know how to dance," confessed the young lady.

Jake stood there with his best poker face. Finally, he spoke, "Well we can right that problem pronto."

"Clara used to say I was the best Virginia Reeler she ever knew," stated the rancher proudly.

"You can teach me?" asked Libby.

"Yes, ma'am," said Jake with a smile. "You'll be able to dance that clod-hopper off'n his feet."

Mrs. Jackson laughed at the rancher's response, as she poured him a cup of coffee. Libby sat down at the table with Jake as he drank his coffee.

Libby looked at Jake with almost sad eyes. "Do you think he's okay?"

"Sure, Ben might be a little thick 'tween the ears, but he's a good fella."

"No, not him. Jake, do you think Chris is all right?"

"I reckon," answered the rancher.

Then in a tone Jake had never heard the girl use before, she said, "I miss him. I wish he was here."

The rancher became concerned. "Didn't you have a good time with the Hawkins' boy today?"

"Yea, it was fun, but...

"But what, honey?" asked Jake.

"Well, oh, nothing," said Libby as she got up from the table to go to her room.

"Whoa!" said Jake. "You can be sure Christian Daniels can take care of himself," reassured the rancher.

Libby smiled, a faint half-hearted one. "Thanks, Jake. Good-night Mrs. Jackson, Jake."

"Good night dearie," returned Mrs. Jackson.

Libby entered her room and shut the door.

"Can you believe that?" Goin' to a dance with a nice young fella and yet, worrying about that old war horse," said the rancher, amazed at the girl.

"You know, Jake," began Mrs. Jackson, "there's no fool like an old one."

Jake was surprised at her response, but said nothing as she left the room. "Wimmen! Ya jest never know which way they're comin' from."

The next morning, Libby helped Mrs. Jackson work on a dress for her to wear to the dance with Ben.

It rained for two days straight. As the sun came out on the third day, Ben drove up. The young man asked Libby to walk with him and she did.

When they returned from their walk, Ben hitched up the buggy and they went for a drive. Maybell had supper ready when they returned.

Ben told of another family moving in next to their land. This made Jake growl, "More squatters!"

"Oh," said Libby, ignoring Jake. "where did they come from?"

"South of here," began Ben. "A small town named Diamond Back. They passed two settlements burned out by raiders."

This got Jake's full attention. "Boy, did they know how long ago those towns got hit?"

"No, sir," answered Ben truthfully. "They said both settlements were still smoking, when they got there."

"Indians?" asked Jake.

"No sir, said they thought it was a man named Coulter and his his gang."

"DAMN!!" shouted Jake slamming his fist on the table. "They give you any idea, why they thought it was Coulter?" continued the rancher.

"No, sir, apparently it was just rumors. They said Coulter has burned out seven or eight towns in the territory, and guess what?" finished the boy.

Before anyone could say anything, Ben continued. "They found a wagon train! Totally wiped out by Coulter and his gang!" Ben grew excited in telling this latest news. "That gang wiped out the WHOLE train! Every man, woman and child was kilt!"

Jake reached out and grabbed Libby's hand as the color quickly faded from her face. The young woman's lips began to quiver as the terror she had survived returned.

"Ben! That'll be enough!" ordered Jake angrily. "You've upset the womenfolk," he explained

Ben turned to Libby and tried to apologize. Before he could speak, tears welled in Libby's eyes and she left the table. Mrs. Jackson followed Libby from the table.

Ben turned to find an enraged Jake glaring at him. "Boy, you best be headin' home," said Jake through gritted teeth.

"I didn't aim to git her so upset," said Ben confused by the turn of events in the last few minutes.

"Ben! Go home!" commanded the rancher.

"All right, all right, I'm gone," said Ben even more confused. "Tell Libby I'll see her tomorrow," said the young lad as an afterthought.

"Best not, wait and see her the night of the dance," suggested Jake.

"Good night, Mr. Karcher. I'll see Libby Saturday."

As Jake closed the door, he thought how lucky Ben had been, "If Chris had been at that table, he'd of ripped out the kid's tongue with his bare hands."

Mrs. Jackson returned shortly. "She's asleep now, but she's pretty upset, and..."

"And what?" snapped the rancher.

"Well, she misses Mr. Daniels."

"Well, nothing," answered Jake. "You can bet he's missing

her too."

The days before the dance seemed to drag by. Libby was more her old self as the dance grew near. Jake had kept his word and with Maybell Jackson's help Libby could barn dance with the best of them by Saturday.

When not serving as dance teacher, Jake was busy putting the Karcher Ranch back on it's feet. He fixed the rose trellis in front of the house. He took a post hole digger and fixed the fences of the corral.

On Friday afternoon, Jake stopped post hold digging long enough for a drink of cool water that Libby had brought him. Wiping the sweat from his brow with the back of his hand he said, "That damn gunslinger of yourn ever show his ass around here again, I'm gonna put him to work doing this."

Libby only grinned at Jake. As hard as his words had sounded, she had learned that Jake thought very highly of her friend.

Jake began carrying in water early Saturday morning. Mrs. Jackson met him at the door, "Good Lord, Man! You've got enough water in here to bath the entire town. Let alone one girl.

"Woman, what do you mean 'one girl'! You surely ain't planning on going without washing are you?" Before the widow could answer, Jake continued. "You don't expect them townfolks to think me a heathen by goin' to the party without my yearly bath!"

Mrs. Jackson was speechless. Libby laughed and offered to help Mrs Jackson prepare for the dance.

Jake went out to fetch some more water. Maybell looked at Libby. "Well how do you like that, I just got asked to the barn dance too. I think?"

Libby laughed again, and so did Mrs. Jackson.

By mid-afternoon the threesome was ready for the trip to town. Ben came by within the quarter hour and picked up Libby in the buggy.

Jake went to the barn and brought out the surrey that he'd bought for Clara on their twenty-fifth wedding anniversary.

The Hawkins came by before the rancher and Mrs. Jackson left for town. Otto Hawkins nodded and bid them good afternoon. Libby Hawkins seemed so excited. 'This is sure gonna be a big day for your youngun'"

The Hawkins wagon continued toward town.

Jake looked to Maybell, but neither had any idea what she

was talking about. When they reached town, the town was already bustling with activity.

Ben gave Libby a hand down from the buggy. He noticed how pretty she looked. Libby had tied her long golden palomino blonde hair back with a sky blue ribbon. The ribbon matched the color of her sparkling eyes and her well-fitted dress. Libby was a fine looking young lady, and Ben was glad she was his date.

Jake had surprised Libby, shortly before Ben arrived by presenting her with Clara's cameo. It has been Clara's prize possession.

Ben escorted Libby into the barn. Many people were already there. The ladies had each brought a plate of food for refreshment. There were large bowls of cider on the table, and the men had their own cider outside the barn in the back. Children were running everywhere. There was a white bearded man tuning his banjo behind the refreshment table.

Several women and girls came up to Libby and introduced themselves to her. Ben proudly greeted his friends, as Libby stood nearby.

Jake and Maybell arrived shortly after the Hawkins.

By the time the first note was played everyone in town was at the shindig. The men all had to leave their weapons at the door. The sheriff stood there. He was more careful to search for liquor than weapons. Once the music started the children knew to settle down and let their parents enjoy themselves.

Libby danced every dance. After the first dance with Ben she was asked by most of the men there for a dance. She had never experienced such an evening.

Jake and Maybell paused from their dancing long enough for Jake to check on Libby. She was easy to spot with the blonde hair and bright blue dress.

It as the sound of gunfire that brought the dance to a stop. The towns people were terrified to find that they were surrounded by masked men. One of the children in the hayloft yelled that the town was on fire, As the people were herded to a corner in the barn.

The huge twin doors were swung open to expose the town in flames. A horseman entered the barn. He rode slowly, taking a long look at each face of his hostages.

Suddenly, Jake called out, "Coutler, you bastard!"

This drew the horseman attention. Jake stepped forward. Libby was frightened, and horrified when she recognized Coulter. She realized Jake's peril and called to him, but it was too late.

"Karcher!" yelled out the horseman as he charged his horse at the burly rancher.

Jake grabbed at the reins, but Coulter swung his rifle butt at the rancher. There was a loud thud as the wood handle hit soundly against the rancher's head. Instantly the charging horse plowed into the falling man. Maybell Jackson screamed, as she saw Jake drop to the ground.

Libby pulled away from Ben's grip and went to Jake.

One of Coulter's men came in, and grabbed hold of Libby, pulling her to her feet.

Desperately she glanced at Ben for help. He wanted to help, but saw the uselessness of intervenion. He realized that he could do nothing to help the girl.

The sheriff made a dash for the guns, by the door. Coulter's men shot him before he could reach the weapons. The women screamed at the sound of the guns going off. Most of the children were crying.

The outlaw holding Libby grabbed her chin, and tried to force a kiss on her lips. She was able to pull away from him, but he reached out and grabbed her arm. He flung her across the floor. She lost her balance and fell sprawling on the floor.

The fall stunned her. Slowly she shook her head, and sat up with her legs bent under her. The outlaw that had released Libby had grabbed another woman.

Suddenly, Libby felt piercing eyes on her. She glanced in the direction of the door. A man's frame filled the doorway. She could feel his constant stare on her. She froze as she realized who it was standing there. The terror that had filled her body a second before began to fade.

The tall figure walked out of the shadow. She knew there was no need to be afraid anymore. Her courage returned. Even a shadow of a smile crossed her lips. Before she could get to her feet, Christian Daniels was beside her.

"Coulter!" called out this man.

The sound of the voice seemed to drive a shock wave through the body of the horseman. What happened in the next few seconds was too fast to see clearly.

Christian Daniels yelled, "Down, Libby!" As guns began blazing. Coulter drew his gun, but his lifeless body dropped beside Libby. Other guns boomed in a thundering roar.

Daniels dropped to one knee beside Libby and she saw the blood as it ran down his arm. Yet, the guns continued to fire. A bullet whizzed by Libby and Daniels moved even closer to her.

The barn filled with smoke from the gunfire. The men from town had used Daniels gunfire to cover them as they reached their weapons. The sound was deafening. It was hard to breathed in the heavy smoke.

Finally the gunfire died out and an eerie silence filled the crowded barn. Daniels got to his feet and went outside. There was several more volleys of gunfire and then the silence came outside also.

Libby got to her feet and ran for the door. Daniels met her in the doorway. "Chris?" she said, but could not continued as she was wrapped in his arm.

She put her arms around him. He kissed the top of her head, as she tightened her grip on him. Slowly, he led her from the barn.

"Are you all right?" he asked.

"Yes," she answered. Then asked. "And yourself?"

"I'll live." he said, rather matter of factly.

Libby pulled up the skirt of the blue dress and tore off part of her petticoat. She then tied it around the bullet wound on Chris's arm.

As he sat there on the hitch rail while she bandaged his arm, he looked at her. It was as though he was seeing the young woman for the first time. She had just finished tying the bandage when he engulfed her in his arms, and kissed her. Finally he released her.

Libby stepped back from Daniels, and he noted the frightened doe look was gone from her eyes. Chris used Libby's shoulder for support as he started to step down from the hitch rail.

Two men were carrying Jake out. Maybell was walking beside him, holding his hand in hers. Doctor Jones was coming behind them. They made a place outside for Jake to rest. The town had burned to the ground.

"Doc, how is he?" inquired Daniels.

"I don't know. It doesn't look good."

Some time later Jake began to move. Shortly. He opened his eyes. "That bastard where is he?" shouted Jake, holding his head.

"He's dead, Jake," answered the gunfighter.

"Damn good riddance!" stated the rancher, still holding his head. "Libby?" Where's the girl?"

"I'm here, Jake," spoke the young woman.

Jake spoke again, over the protest of the doctor. "Chris, I'm damn glad you got back here. You got that bastard Coulter this time! Thank you, my friend."

Daniels said nothing. He nodded that this long unfinished job was now done. The rancher seemed to be at peace now and closed his eyes to rest.

Libby flashed a horrified glance at Chris. He smiled and said, "No, he's not dead. He'll be fine."

"Let me check your injury," said the doctor to Daniels. As the doctor cleaned and bandaged the wound on Daniels arm, Ben Hawkins drove up in the buggy.

"Libby, I'm sorry," he began. "There just wasn't nothing I could do."

"I know," said Libby with her disappointment obvious.

"I'm ready to drive you home," continued Ben.

Libby turned from watching the doctor bandaging Daniels arm and faced the younger man. "Thank you Ben, but I'm needed here," she stated.

"But Libby, I got something to ask you," pleaded young Hawkins.

"No!" snapped Libby. "I'm not leaving with you!"

Daniels interrupted. "Go ahead Libby. I'll bring Jake home." If he's able."

"But..." hesitated the girl.

"Go on," motioned Daniels.

Ben helped Libby into the buggy. She turned and watched Daniels as the buggy pulled away.

It took Ben sometime to build up the courage to speak. "Libby," he said. "Ma said you could wear her wedding dress."

"What??!" asked the young woman.

"When we marry," began Ben. "You can look like my mother when she married Pa." Nervously finished Ben as he pulled the buggy to a stop. Libby looked at him.

"Libby, will you marry me?" he asked.

The girl looked at him, surprised at his proposal. Then with little emotion she said, "Ben," I don't love you. You are a very dear friend, but I don't want to marry you."

"Ma said you might not say yes right away, but I'll wait." stated the young man in almost a relieved tone.

"Ben," began the young woman. "There is only one man I 'would' marry."

It's that killer Daniels, ain't it!" accused Ben rudely. "Ma said she thought you were sweet on him!"

"That's enough, Ben!" said Libby angrily.

"Well he ain't the marrying kind," announced Ben. "He'd never marry you!"

"That's enough Ben Hawkins!" She said angrily, getting out of the buggy.

"Well its the truth! He won't marry you!" yelled Ben as he drove away in the buggy.

Libby picked up a clod of dirt and flung it at the departing buggy. She heard a noise and was startled by the horse and rider behind her. Color rushed to her face. In the light of the full moon her face seemed to glow.

Christian Daniels was sitting there on the little grullo. The gunman sat there with his bad arm resting on the saddlehorn. Still upset and angry by all the events of the evening, she asked, "Well, I guess you heard all that!"

He kicked his foot out of the stirrup and extended his hand to her. Ignoring her remark, he said, "Com' on git on. It's a long walk to Jake's."

She swung up behind him. It took her several minutes to get her dress situated so she was sitting comfortably. The mustang then headed home.

They traveled just a short distance when he felt her rest her head on his shoulder. Less than a quarter mile down the road he felt her head start to slip to the side. Gently he pulled the mustang up. Then with a little dexterity he dismounted and let her slide off the horse and into his arm.

She never woke up. He held her and stepped back into the saddle. He sat her sidesaddle in the saddle seat and he sat on the bedroll behind the saddle. She leaned against him as he gently eased the horse back on the trail.

The grullo walked slowly picking his step carefully.

When they arrived at Jake's Christian Daniels gently nudged her awake. "Angel, were home," he said.

Drowsily she slid out of the saddle. "Chris..." she said wiping the sleep from her eyes.

"Yea..." he answered as he slid off the mustang, and loosened the cinch.

"You saved my life, again," she stated.,

"Uh, huh," answered the man trying to avoid the conversation.

"Chris," she began again, still very sleepy.

"What?" he asked.

"Why do you think..." she stopped and announced. "I'm going in and go to bed."

Daniels laughed to himself. Times like this she was cute as a button and he just loved her. Coulter and his men seemed a million years ago. Daniels smiled as he thought of the way she'd picked up the clod of dirt and flung it after the Hawkin's buggy.

Daniels pulled the saddle off the weary horse and turned him into the corral with the Percheron. As he reached down to pick up his saddle he felt the sharp pain in his arm from the bullet wound. He had ignored the throbbing pain, but it was letting him know it now.

He went into the kitchen and lit the lamp on the table. He then filled the basin with water to soak the injury. The wound was bleeding again through the doctor's bandage and down his arm. He took his shirt off and unwrapped the bandage and began putting water on the wound.

"Let me help!" came a voice from the darkness.

Daniels looked up. The voice was familiar, yet different. Libby came into the light. She had on a flannel nightgown and her hair was down over her shoulders.

She knelt beside his chair and placed cold rags on his arm. Her touch was soft and soothing. She stood up and fetched the salve from the cupboard and rubbed the wound heavily with the salve. She then rebandaged his arm. "There, that ought to keep it till morning, she said.

"Thanks," said Daniels.

"Is Jake doing all right?" she asked.

"Yeah, but Doc didn't think he oughta travel tonight," answered the gunman.

"Chris," she began hesitantly. "I'm sure glad your back. I missed you," she confessed.

"Well that makes two of us," answered Daniels honestly. "I'm sure glad I'm back."

Libby poured him a cup of coffee and sat down on the other side of the table. "Chris, we just have to talk," she began.

He looked at her, with one of those soul piercing glances that could see right through her. He said with an angry tone, "I told you before, if you got something to say, say it!"

"You'll think this is silly," she began as color rushed to her face. "I don't want you to leave me again. I missed you so."

"Angel," he began earnestly. "I got no right to you. I'm nearly twice as old as you, and I've made enemies. People that don't forget easy. There's a bullet out there with my name on it," he stated.

Putting her hands to her ears, she spoke, "Don't talk like that!" "I can't lose you too!"

Angrily Daniels reached over and grasped each of her forearms in his hands. "Listen to me! You mean more to me than anything ever has, but that don't change how life is. I can't make my past go away. When I found you...it was the luckiest day of my life. You needed me, and I liked being needed."

Then shaking his head he continued, "But, I can't keep you from living a normal life. I got no right!"

"Chris..I love you!" she said with feeling and emotion controlling her words.

"Love!?" he said mocking her words. "You loved Brother Zebadiah," he accused.

She sprang from her chair as she shouted, "That's a lie!!! I hated him!!"

Angrily he accused, "Well you sure had a strange way of showing it. If I hadn't come back you'd been wedded and bedded!"

"NEVER!!" she shouted in anger. "After he hit me, I'da killed myself first!"

A sudden change came over Daniels, "When'd he hit you?"

"It doesn't matter," she said.

"What the hell, you mean, 'it doesn't matter'? Nobody lays a hand on you!"

She smiled. Then she said, "We've had a long day. Good night, Chris."

"Night, Libby," said Christian Daniels.

Libby went to her room. Daniels did not turn in right away. He sat at the kitchen table and finished his coffee. His arm was sore and he treated it carefully.

Libby had been asleep sometime when she was awakened by rough hands. "Angel, put these on," said the familiar voice she'd grown to love.

"Chris?" she asked as she did as he requested. "Where we goin'?"

"Does it matter?" he asked.

"No," she answered honestly.

"We're getting married! Now, get a move on!"

"Chris?" she asked in disbelief.

"Aw hell, Angel!" he said. "There's a hundred reasons why we shouldn't but I Do LOVE YOU, Libby!" he confessed.

"Chris," she said as he grabbed her up in his arms and kissed her passionately. She returned his kisses.

He pulled away from her arms and with a swat to her butt he said, "Now get dressed 'fore we get the cart before the horse!"

Libby grinned at him as she finished pulling up the trousers he had brought for her to wear.

Daniels went outside, and Libby followed him shortly. She waited as Chris saddled the little mustang. Once again, Daniels put her in the saddle and swung up behind her.

"You know, I can't make you no promises about what's ahead. Except that I'll love you till the end of time and beyond."

"I don't care about what's ahead...so long as I'm with you," said Libby.

Daniels tightened his grip on the reins and in so doing tightened his grip on the girl.